REMY SNEAKERS

AND THE LOST TREASURE

ALSO BY KEVIN SHERRY

Remy Sneakers vs. the Robo-Rats

The Yeti Files series:
Meet the Bigfeet
Monsters on the Run
Attack of the Kraken

REMY SNEAKERS
AND THE LOST TREASURE

KEVIN SHERRY

SCHOLASTIC PRESS / NEW YORK

To Ed Schrader

Library of Congress Cataloging-in-Publication Data available

ISBN 978-1-338-03461-5

10 9 8 7 6 5 4 3 2 1   18 19 20 21 22

Printed in the U.S.A. 23

First edition, May 2018

Book design by Carol Ly and Baily Crawford

Chapter 1
MISSING TREASURE

Once again, trouble was brewing for Remy Sneakers.

Someone broke into my home!

My cables have been cut.

My jars have been jostled.

My marbles are all mixed-up.

My treasures have been battered and scattered!

Is anything missing?

I'm not sure.

The one thing I care about most is in a secret spot.

I hope it's still there!

5

From when I was just a cub.

My grandma would tell me and my cousins the most amazing stories about our family and our woodland home.

And my grandpa would draw pictures in his journal so we'd remember the stories.

RACHEL

REMY

But then the bulldozers came.

They chased us out of the woods.

We had to run for our lives. But I couldn't leave Grandpa's journal behind. It held too many memories!

By the time I got hold of it, my family had scattered to the winds. I escaped to the city and never looked back.

That journal was special. That's why I locked it up. And I always carry the key with me.

But now that it's gone, the only way I'll remember Grandpa's face is to draw it myself. I just wish I was better at it.

Wait . . . who are you?

I'm Buttercup.
I've seen you around the neighborhood.
And I'll tell you what you should be drawing
if you ever want to find your journal.

The thief who stole it!

C'MON, draw its long, pointed snout.

And its tiny little arms.

And its long, scaly tail.

We're friends, aren't we?

Uh, we hardly know each other.

And since we're friends, you could repay my kindness with a few of the shiny trinkets in your fanny pack...

Hey! Get your paws off!

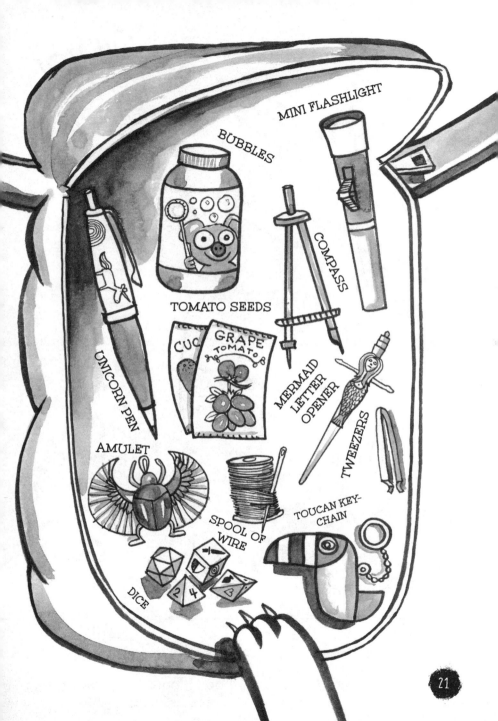

MINI FLASHLIGHT

BUBBLES

COMPASS

TOMATO SEEDS

CUC

GRAPE
TOMATO

UNICORN PEN

MERMAID
LETTER
OPENER

TWEEZERS

AMULET

SPOOL OF
WIRE

TOUCAN KEY-
CHAIN

DICE

It seemed Remy had been tricked.

If you want to get by me and my friends, you'll have to pay a toll.

You can keep the key. But we'll take everything else you've got.

25

So Remy handed over his loot and got out his pencil.

Chapter 3

BENEATH THE STREETS

I think I know where we can find the thief. Follow me.

Uh . . . nice to meet you. Big Al is it? I'm not really with the raccoon, I swear. These guys paid me to take them on a sewer tour. But I'm just like you—only looking out for myself. You wouldn't hurt a fellow businessman, would you, Big Al?

THE PITS

STOP IT RIGHT NOW!

Fighting isn't going to get us out of here. For better or worse, we're in this mess together.

I'M SO SORRY.

I let my cat friends take your stuff.
I thought if I helped you snag the journal I could make
it up to you. But I shouldn't have brought us down here.

I believe him, Torch.

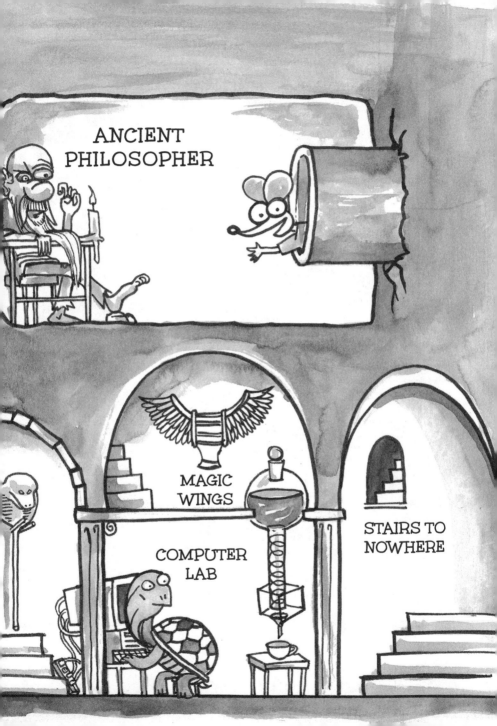

Hurry! If we get out of here, I'll never take a shortcut again!

C'mon, Critter Crew. We've got this!

Chapter 5

WORKING TOGETHER

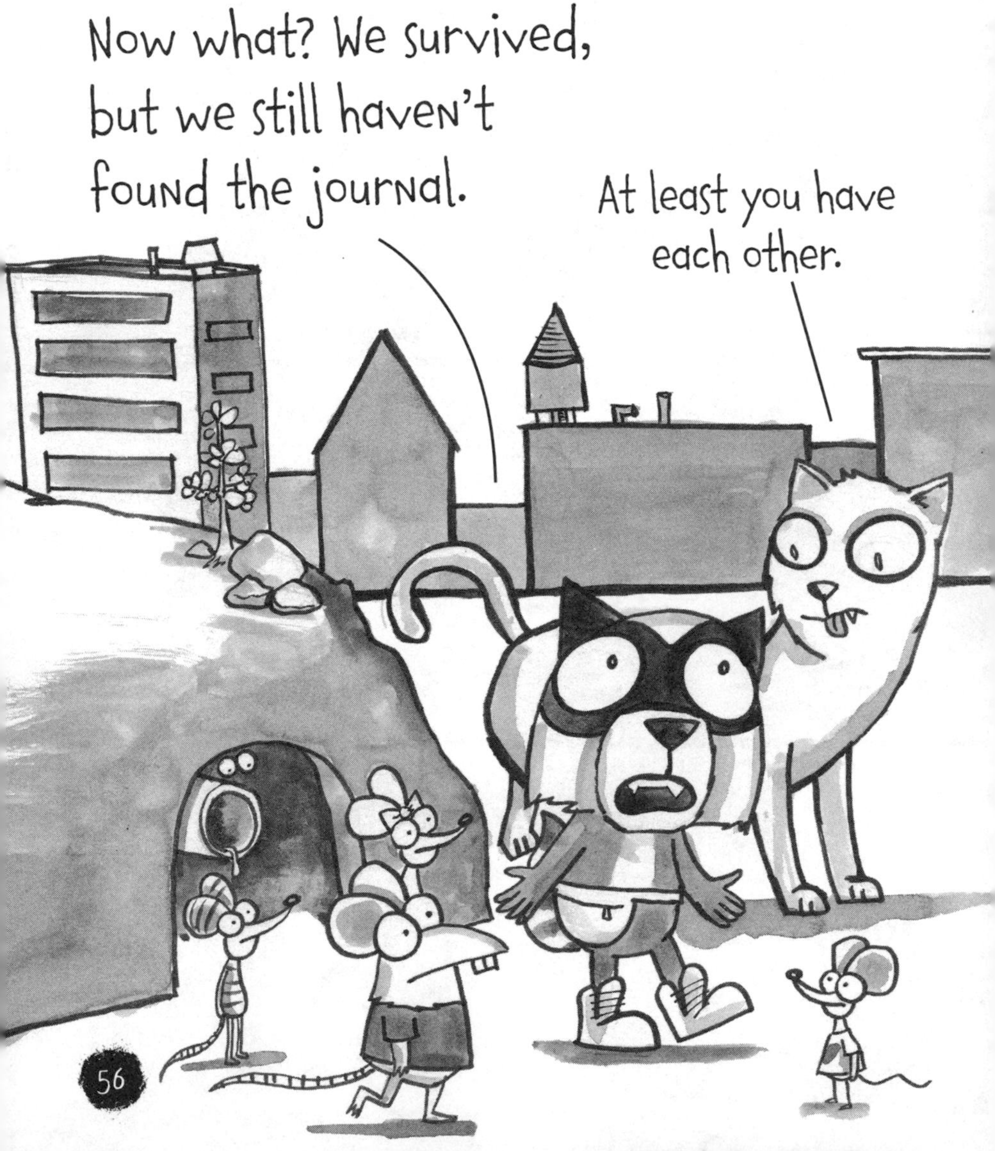

I really am sorry, Torch.
I hope someday we can be friends.

Are you kidding? You risked your life for me. And you caved in the tunnel on those dirty rats. Of course we're friends.

Good. I've always wanted to be on a team. I guess that's why I let the other cats push me around.

But now I'm part of the Critter Crew!

Thanks! The more I draw, the easier it gets. And it makes me feel closer to my grandpa.

That was so sweet. Your escape was the distraction I needed to sneak away. And since you helped me, I want to help you.

There's a café on the other side of town. Stew's Stump has the best food.

AL'S DEN

RIPE DUMPSTER

HUGE TRUCKS

QUICKSAND

GLOWING BARRELS

EMPTY BUILDINGS

STU'S STUMP

You might find a clue about your journal there.

That map was SO helpful! Do you see that stump with the symbols on it? The entrance to the café is behind it. But I've heard some pretty tough characters hang around this place.

Cool Disguises

Grrr!

Hiya!

65

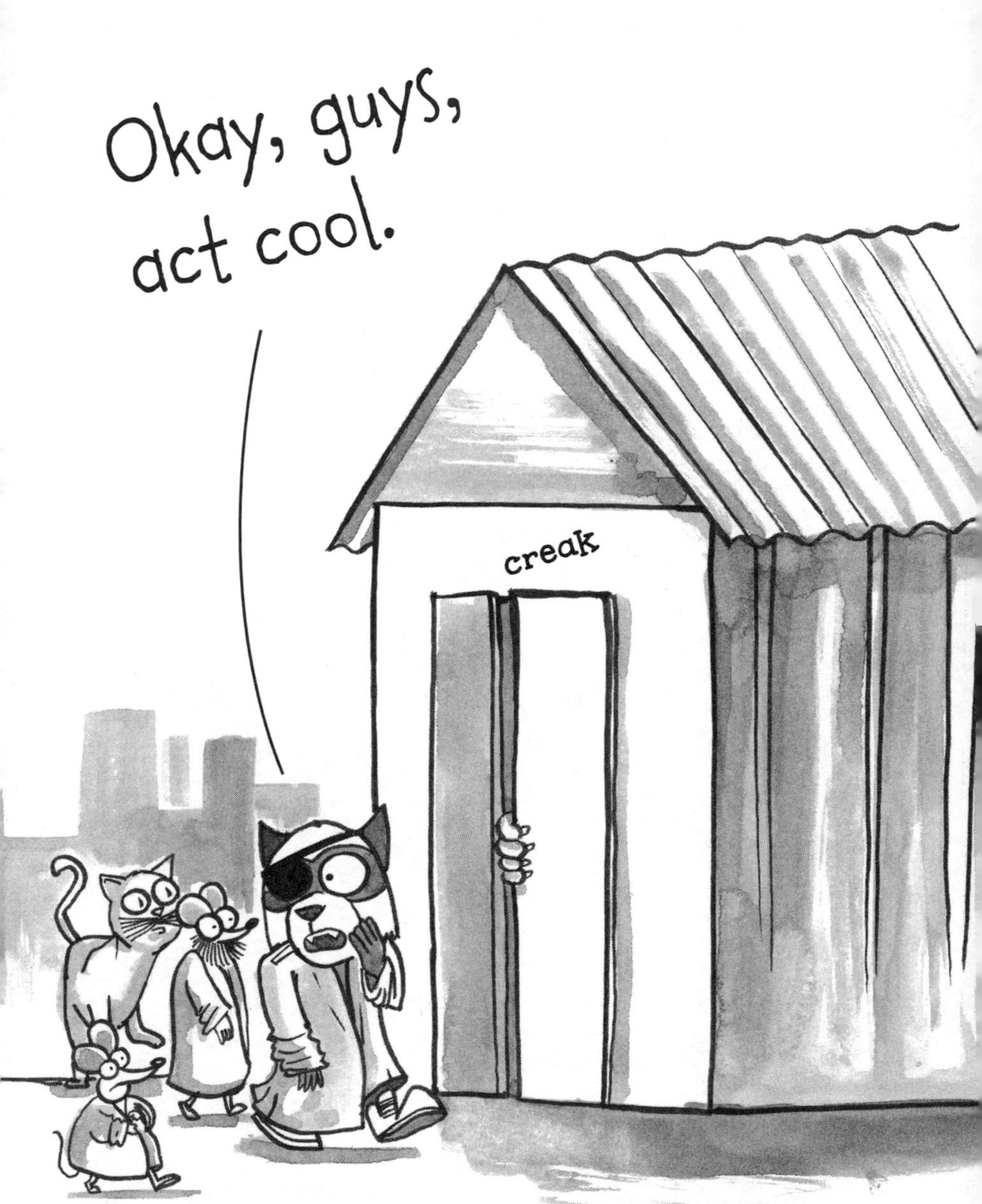
Okay, guys, act cool.
creak

Um . . . we don't actually have the password per se . . . but my buddy Remy will draw your picture if you let us in.

Do you like surfing? Sure you do. You'd look pretty cool on a board.

Inside, the Critter Crew found the café packed with suspicious-looking creatures.

Have You Seen a Furry Alligator?

No way!

S-s-sounds s-s-strange.

Are you selling insurance?

Get outta here!

Nope.

Who's asking?

Chapter 6

THE FURRY GATOR

Psst, Remy. That's him. That's the furry gator I saw. And there are two of them!

A possum is an American marsupial. That means it carries its young in a pouch.

FOXTROT 1:12 P.M.
lilipedia.org
possum

The possum is found throughout North America.

Okay, let's make a plan to confront them. First we should—

Stop!

Yeah, so what? We steal for a living. And we're good at it.

Anyone with the cash can hire us to do a job.

Shiny! I want it!

The game is on! Whoever draws the most impressive picture wins.

And it better be me, because I CAN'T lose that key.

Gimme that! I'll draw a big pair of boots to stomp on your flowers.

Well, I'll make your boots fancy.

Not even a steaming hot bubble bath with bonbons, your favorite book, and lavender bath salts for your tired marsupial muscles?

That sounds amazing!

Chapter 7

THE GREAT CHASE

The Critter Crew took off after the thief.

If we work together, we can catch her!

Ra raced through the warehouse district. She led the crew toward the noisy rumble of the subway and darted inside the tunnel.

WARNING: This story is going sideways! (Turn the book.)

RUMBLE

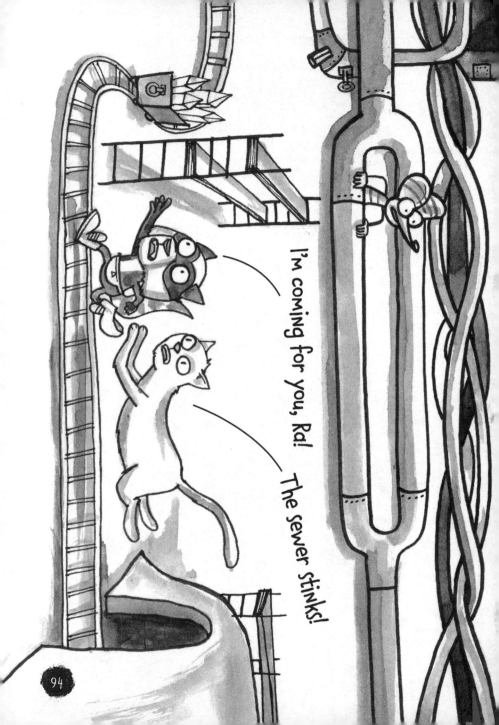

Turn the book back!

Watch out!

She's getting away!

Ra easily leapt onto a fire escape . . .

WHOOSH

. . . but it was too high for the Critter Crew.

97

Remy, if you jump on my back, you can reach the ladder.

Oh no! I can't fail now. Looks like I need to get creative!

Chapter 8
REUNITED

We must be related! But the journal is locked . . .

I have the key!

Raccoon
Family Tree

I wanted a piece of our family back. I didn't realize YOU were that family.

UNTIE

Cousin Rachel?

113

The Critter Crew's hunt for

a lost treasure.

Just think about how you're feeling, what you want most in the world, or great memories you want to hold on to.
Then pick up a pencil and draw them.

REMY

FRIENDLY
NEIGHBORHOOD
BEAVER

REMY DOESN'T
LIKE TO SWIM!

RACHEL IS
A NATURAL
CLIMBER!

IDEAS FOR TOWER RENOVATIONS

RACHEL

MAP TO OUR FAVORITE MULBERRY TREE

Yes, you do. We're all family now. You can stay with me while we fix your place. We'll make some new memories together, and start a new journal.

Thanks, Rachel. It'll take a while to rebuild my collections.

DON'T MISS REMY'S FIRST EXCITING ADVENTURE!

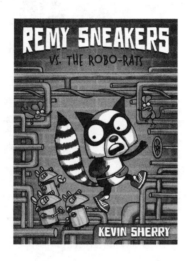

Remy Sneakers is not a thief!

To clear his name, Remy needs some help from the city critters . . . but mice, rats, and pigeons are not exactly best buds. They will have to band together if they want to stop the real criminal mastermind and save their city from total destruction by an army of robo-rodents!

ABOUT THE AUTHOR

Kevin Sherry is the author and illustrator of many children's books, most notably The Yeti Files series and *I'm the Biggest Thing in the Ocean*, which received starred reviews and won an original artwork award from the Society of Illustrators. He's a man of many interests: a chef, a cyclist, an avid screen printer, and a performer of hilarious puppet shows for kids and adults. Kevin lives in Baltimore, Maryland.

ACKNOWLEDGMENTS

Huge thanks to Teresa Kietlinki, Brian, Erin Nutsugah, Dan Deacon, Bill Stevenson, John Clinton, Matt Farley, and my mom and dad.